TO NORA, ONE MORE TIME

*"It's a poor sort of memory that only works backwards,"*

*the Queen remarked.*

—— LEWIS CARROLL

*These fragments I have shored against my ruins.*

—— T. S. ELIOT

I wasn't going to begin again, having stopped, apparently, and started up again, foolishly, too many times already, attempting to write about my family and Spring Hope and myself there with them and later there without them.

Writing a few pages and giving up.

Between one stopping and another starting there was always an interlude, filled in its first part by regret at having stopped and in its second part by excitement at starting again, finally, and I tried to write about that too once, or maybe twice, I don't remember, a tragicomic tale of my endeavors to write that other thing, this one to be titled *Pendulum.*

Or *Oscillation,* to avoid associations with Poe.

And wrote several more pages that I filed away with the rest.

Rejecting the temptation to lay them out on the floor and scribble all over them with a big red crayon, the way I used to scribble over my drawings when I was a child and they refused to look the way I wanted.

Scribbled them out, crumpled them into little balls, then threw myself down on the carpet and screamed.

My mother would say, "Do you think Matisse lay on the carpet and screamed when he was your age?"

I have sparrows on my window ledge this morning. I don't have a hairbrush.

I don't know who lives at Spring Hope now.

I have never liked Poe.

Truth is, despite my many failures and despite what I told myself, I have never actually stopped searching. In some deep recess of mind, in my heart of hearts—a phrase my mother loved—I never abandoned all hope.

As people once had to in the Dante poem, supposedly, before entering hell, of which I could recite the first lines from memory, I believe, in Italian, when I was quite small.

"Now Eve will recite the first lines of *The Divine Comedy* by Dante Alighieri," my mother said, I imagine.

The objects of my pursuit were figments, mental images, and phantasms. I would refer to these figments, etc., as Mama, Papa, my mother, my father, our mother, my brothers, Spring Hope, the dog Gracie, the coal bin, the chinaberry tree by the tractor barn, and so forth, talking about them in the same unreflective way that I speak today of this room, this desk, Maria, Lester, and so forth.

They are figments now, I mean.

*Searching* is not really the word for what I do, have been doing for a long time, since I know where they are, where the images and memories of my mother and so forth are, and can't search for them, properly speaking, there, meaning in my head or mind or whatever, soul even, where they lie very quiet, lost or buried in the darkness there or in the brightness, though it is the right word for my attempts to find the hairbrush.

One would not say, for example, while breathing into the mouth of a person who has drowned and is not at all breathing that one is searching for life there.

I wanted to breathe life back into the memories that had drowned there, in the darkness of the mind, as I said, or soul.

*Resuscitate* is the word for that, for what I tried to do many times over the years, and stopped, and finally almost lost hope of ever doing successfully, as I said.

I remember aiming a jet of water from a garden hose into a hole at the base of a large oak tree and being surprised when a toad hopped out.

I remember a woman we called Miss Henrietta, who was extremely tall and thin, seated in a very small chair reading to us at school, and wishing I was home.

I remember Thornton dropping a tick into the mouth of a pitcher plant and saying, "Look, now it's digesting it," but the tick was just swimming around.

I remember my hair full of dirt and twigs. I remember my father telling me to bathe. I remember that I wouldn't change my clothes. I remember listening to Wagner on my record player as loud as I could make it go.

The hairbrush I used to have has disappeared mysteriously. Maria thinks it fell off the window ledge into the bushes.

There is always birdseed on the window ledge. I said to her, "Do you think I would put my brush in the birdseed?"

Maria is forty-seven years old and believes in magic. She has believed in magic since she was a child, when her mother saw the Virgin standing on the roof of a church.

It was a Mexican church, of course.

I say "of course" because Mexico is a thoroughly magical place, Thornton and Silvia discovered when they traveled there.

I personally have never traveled to Mexico.

Connecticut is the most distant place I have traveled to. My mother traveled to Boston, New York, and Chicago. My father traveled to Brazil and Argentina. Thornton has traveled to England, Japan, and the Philippines, at least, in addition to Mexico. I can't imagine where Edward might have traveled to by now, if he has traveled at all.

First Edward, then Thornton, then me.

I remember a big square high-ceilinged box of a house, dim and almost cool on hot afternoons when the louvered shutters were pulled over the windows, and ice cold in winter when the only heat was from coal grates in the fireplaces, and that had been white once but displayed vastly more gray weathered wood than paint all the time I lived there.

I remember as a young girl saying to myself, "I am Eve Annette Trezevant Taggart of Spring Hope," half pretending I was an old-world aristocrat, and then looking around, embarrassed, fearing I had spoken it aloud.

Even now—especially now, I suppose—I can be sitting quietly, unaware that I am even thinking at all, and suddenly I'll hear my own voice so loud it makes me jump.

Other times, Maria will look over at me and ask, "What did you say?" and I'll know that I was muttering.

I remember my mother at her desk writing and muttering to herself also.

For a long time I thought that just being here, the physical distance from Spring Hope, would allow me to resuscitate Papa and my brothers and my mother and her famous notebooks and all the dogs and Spring Hope itself, the entire past just as it was, lying apparently lifeless in the darkness within, in the damp and fog, so to speak, as I also pictured it sometimes.

Even though there is very little solitude here. Maria is here much of the day, or Lester is here, even when I don't need him. Sometimes they are both here, all three of us in a row on the sofa watching television.

And there is also the fear that once started, I won't be able to stop.

My mother's name was Iris.

That being the name both of a woman who was born in the first part of the twentieth century in South Carolina, in the southern portion of the United States, and lived and died in the so-called real world, and of a phantasm of no fixed or definite shape that draws and clusters to itself a host of other images like filings to a magnet. This phantasm was born with the first opening of my mind onto the world and will die with me, finally.

Wild irises called blue flags bloomed every spring in the ditches that lined both sides of the narrow rutted lane that ran in from the highway to the house, and in the boggy places in the woods, and along the edges of the dikes, but I don't know if they were the reason she was named Iris, though she was born at Spring Hope in April.

I remember my father, in canvas jacket and rubber boots, coming through the door of the house with an armful of blue flags for her birthday.

She once told me that the blue parts of her eyes were called irises because they were the color of the flowers and that the same parts of my brown eyes were called mushrooms.

Before the blue flags I remember the red sorrel that we called sour grass, that grew in abandoned fields and that we chewed on for the tangy sour flavor.

Which is the second-oldest memory I have of any kind of taste.

The oldest, I believe, being the taste of a penny when I was two.

Even today, if I hear someone say that something or other possesses a metallic taste, I notice on my tongue the flavor of a penny.

That flavor being another of the memory-items, so to speak, that cling to the figment of my mother and my mother's finger reaching into my mouth to extract the penny.

Later a great many of my memories are of words. I remember, for example, the first time I heard the words *menstrual cramps,* though I don't remember the first time I had menstrual cramps.

I have an image of Mama's dresser and my child-self seated on a satin-covered stool in front of it while Mama brushes my hair. The fabric on the stool is decorated with red, blue, and yellow tropical birds and is frayed around the edges, I can see.

Watching her in the mirror while she brushes with long vigorous strokes that I have to strain against to keep my head from being jerked backwards.

Feeling it still, when I think about it, in the muscles of my neck, remembering it there.

She stops in mid-stroke, hovering the brush above my head. My hair makes a crackling noise and floats up to it. "Electricity," she says.

I remember "You Live Better Electrically" in large italic letters on the back of a magazine beneath a picture of a young woman in a tiny ruffled apron smiling down at a gleaming white electric cook-stove on which someone has drawn a big red valentine heart, in lipstick we are supposed to think.

Lila, and Mama when she was in the kitchen, wore long white bib aprons with pockets.

I remember calling the burners on an electric stove *eyes.* Everyone I knew called them that when I was a child, while almost no one does now. Even people who have never left the South have stopped calling them eyes. I stopped without really meaning to, it was just that one day I began to say *burner* instead.

Thinking about that this morning, at the stove waiting for the kettle to boil.

The mirror had a wooden frame of carved acanthus leaves. I remember knowing that it was very old and had belonged to my grandmother. Several of the leaves were chipped or broken off and there were black spots and speckles in the glass.

The dresser lamps, one at each end, had tasseled shades and tall fluted bases of blue-tinted glass. I remember Mama telling me that years of sunlight falling through the large windows on either side of the dresser had tinted the glass that pale blue.

I was an adult before I learned that this was not true.

The windows had white muslin curtains that lifted and floated in the slightest breeze, like ghosts, I remember thinking then, the same kind of curtains I have on my windows here.

No image remains of my grandmother. A fox-fur stole is the only bit of enduring figment I am able to attach to the word *grandmother*. This matching pair of fox pelts complete with glass-eyed heads and bushy tails must have produced on me an impression so dazzling it has completely obliterated the face of the woman around whose neck they once dangled, and what floats above them now is a visage-less oval, like the featureless face of a certain type of department store mannequin.

I remember a framed reproduction of *Whistler's Mother* hanging on a wall in my mother's bedroom above a blanket chest that smelled of mothballs when you opened it.

I remember thinking the severe-looking seated figure in black was a picture of my grandmother, and being disappointed when I found out it wasn't.

I remember always knowing that mothballs were poisonous.

Now that I am at my desk again for more time than it takes to write a postcard, I am fond of mornings in particular, especially when the sky is clear and the white of the building across the way is splashed with sunlight, splashing back onto my face.

Writing on typing paper in pencil. A little something, even if only a sketch.

Resolving to be wary of the false objectivity of words, having learned from my failures, hauling something to the surface and having words batter it beyond recognition.

The desk stood beneath a much larger window at Spring Hope in a downstairs room we called the library.

Spring Hope was the only house I have ever been in that had a room called a library.

With the door closed I barely hear the television in the kitchen. With the window open, as it is now, I have the sound of a marching band practicing somewhere far off, birds singing, and the usual noise of traffic and people from the avenue at the end of a narrow passageway three stories below.

The subdued murmur or rumble is quite pleasant, even reassuring at times, being the sound of busy people going hither and thither on the errands of life, as I think of it sometimes.

A busy, busy world that I have never been quite entirely a part of.

The window has not been fitted with bars. Obviously no one, meaning none of the people who constructed this building, expected someone to jump out of it, though I might in fact jump out of it.

Having considered jumping from here, and from other windows in places I inhabited in the past, and from rooftops, as well, on the two occasions I climbed up on one of those.

It is amazing that I have reached the age I have with all four limbs, not to mention other even more vital segments, reasonably intact.

Without including here the so-called normal and expected alterations to my person that are usually grouped under the rubric *ravages of time.*

I once wrote an entire book that I called *A History of My Suicides.*

It was a work of fiction, of course.

I am quite old, it feels to me now, older than my mother was when she died.

Her last years spent in another room with this desk, a larger room with tall windows and muslin curtains.

I am quite like her in appearance, I believe, more so as I age, becoming gaunt, as she was.

Calling it a desk gives a wrong impression, I am sure, summoning images of a squarish, practical sort of item. It is actually a delicate Chippendale desk, rather like a small table, with elegantly curved spindly legs and a pair of shallow drawers fitted with ormolu pulls hanging from the jaws of escutcheon lions. It was my mother's desk and it is the only piece of furniture I have from Spring Hope.

I haven't used the desk for writing before. It is too rickety to type on and for many years typing was the only manner of transcribing thoughts and images that I felt suitable to the fluid and rapid progression of those thoughts and images across the clearing in my mind that I, following what I believe is standard usage among philosophers, mean to indicate with the word *consciousness.*

Only since living here have I used it for writing— not because I think writing in longhand will make a difference, though I do think it might make a difference, but because it was my mother's desk and sitting at it I feel that I am sitting in for her, so to speak.

Writing at the desk I sometimes get the feeling that I *am* my mother.

I have no idea what the sentence I just wrote means.

I remember my mother reading to me from "The Waste Land": "Darling, it doesn't matter that you don't understand what it means so long as you can *feel* what it means."

We were seated in white wicker armchairs on a side porch at Spring Hope when she said that.

The house had two porches on that side, one above the other, and wisteria vines climbed the columns of the first porch and hung drooping from the banisters on the second.

I don't remember that from when I first knew the porch.

From that time I remember only the green-tinted air on the vine-darkened lower porch. Sunlight penetrated the leaves and cast trembling patterns on the brick floor. I remember ants coming out of a crack between the bricks.

I don't remember when I began to know that there were two porches, that the vine would produce clusters of blue flowers in spring, that it was called wisteria.

I remember the fragrance from the flowers made me dizzy and I was afraid to put my nose close because of bees, but I don't remember the precise moment when those things became so.

Later I learned there was a word in another language for the color of the air on the porch behind the wall of wisteria—*verdâtre*—and now the memory of the air is colored by that word, as if the color of the word had bled on it.

I remember (much later) my mother's collection of lavender dresses.

I have (an imaginary) painting of my imagined mother sitting in a white chair, a wooden white-painted kitchen chair this time, not one of the wicker porch chairs, in the yard at Spring Hope, wearing a lavender dress, in front of a wall of blossoming wisteria that reaches all the way to the top of the frame.

She is sitting up very straight, feet together, hands folded in her lap, the way she did in fact sit often.

I want to say that my mother sat primly, often.

Putting my eyes close to the canvas, so to call it, I see that she is smiling faintly, the way she smiled when downcast, or "in the dumps," as we liked to put it, wanting to minimize or even belittle, when one of us—where by "us" I mean one of her children, not Lila or Papa—would say something we thought cheering or comical or, I suppose, even endearing, not exactly to comfort her so much as to entice her back from whatever place she had wandered off into.

I want to say that in this picture her mind is *elsewhere* and that she is smiling *distantly*.

The painting is called *Portrait of the Artist's Mother with Wisteria,* I think.

And then I think of hysteria, of course.

She dressed in lavender every day and for every occasion except funerals.

People must have thought this predilection for lavender was wildly eccentric, I imagine now, though I don't recall anyone ever mentioning it.

By the time I was old enough to understand what was being said she had become just one more odd thing that people had grown used to, I suppose.

The white chair, the one my mother is sitting on in the picture, was in the kitchen until it broke, and then it was leaning on three legs against the back wall of the chicken house, where the paint curled off it and termites chewed up the feet.

I remember (later) dragging the chair over to the wire incinerator so Verdell could throw it in.

Baudelaire and Mallarmé were crazy about Poe.

Baudelaire and Mallarmé were great writers, supposedly, but they were not very good readers, it seems to me.

Baudelaire, Mallarmé, and Rimbaud all sit together in a little drawer in a corner of my mind, as "French poets I have read a little of."

James McNeill Whistler is also in that drawer, as a friend of Mallarmé's, even though he was not a French poet.

James McNeill Whistler sits with Claude Monet and Michelangelo in another little drawer as well, this one labeled "Painters my mother had books about."

In talking of these people I am of course referring to the memory images of them that I have carried with me from childhood—images and figments that include not just pictures, but words, smells, and so forth—and not to the actual historical persons about whom I could, were I so inclined, find accurate information in an encyclopedia.

The figments and images are not information about anything except the furniture of my memory, and were I to learn tomorrow that Whistler and Mallarmé were not friends, had never encountered each other even once, they would continue to sit together in the same little drawer.

Though I am in fact quite certain that they—meaning now the actual historical persons—really were fond of each other.

I remember thinking Whistler was a funny name for a painter.

None of us thought it funny that Lila's last name was White.

Why is human the name of a race?

I am a member of the human race. I am a member of the National Audubon Society.

If you pronounce Audubon's name in the correct way it sounds funny.

Audubon changed his first name from Jean-Jacques to John James so as not to sound funny, presumably.

I became a member of the human race in 1940.

I became a member of the National Audubon Society in 1951 or 1952, on my birthday.

It was the birthday after the one on which I became a member of the National Geographic Society.

My parents thought of it as nourishing the mind.

The National Audubon Society was not founded by John James Audubon, I found out later, sadly.

Lila's husband was named Alvin Junior.

I don't pay dues to remain a member of the human race.

Standing at the living room window, I watch Maria walk away down the street, a sturdy diminutive woman rendered dwarfish by my height above her, going off with quick, determined steps, a large black handbag cradled in the crook of an arm, a broken strap dangling. A beetle-like shadow creeps at her feet.

Maria is good natured, kind, resilient. She is well equipped for life, I can't help thinking, able to withstand the blows of fate and inclement circumstance, and so forth. She probably can't even imagine herself in the situation of someone like me, who is thoroughly ill equipped, can't imagine wandering in a dark forest as I am, I want to say, constantly, even though it is not like a forest actually, where I would be stumbling into trees, bushes, and so forth, thorny thickets and such, probably. More like a place without boundaries, enveloped in a thick fog, an almost impenetrable vapor, populated by vague shapes that don't become clearer as I approach, a desert, if there can be fog in a desert, rather than a forest.

Sometimes I think of it as the *inner reaches.*

After grocery shopping with Lester, stopping at the drugstore for more paper. Writing a few pages and then filing them away.

The file drawer rolls on little metal wheels and makes a smooth, oily, sinister sound when I pull it out, followed by a rustling of dry leaves as I thumb through the folders. It reminds me of the drawers they keep bodies in at the morgue, on television.

It is half full of my pages.

There are other, empty drawers below that one.

The sentence, "More even than death itself she feared running out of paper."

I remember arriving home long after bedtime and being carried from the car half asleep.

I remember climbing the stairs to my room, dragging my feet as if too tired to take another step, and knowing I was pretending.

I remember pretending to be sick.

The time I thought I was pretending to be sick and then actually became sick.

The discovery, later, that I could actually make myself ill by pretending with sufficient intensity.

The times, much later, when I pretended to be crazy, so people wouldn't know how dull and thoughtless I actually was.

Even today, lying in bed with my eyes closed I can summon the memory of the swaying motion of being carried, a memory so definite, so physically vivid, that if I didn't know better I would assume my bed was gently rocking.

Though perhaps what my body is remembering in this way is not the specific sensation of being carried when I was very small but a much later experience—of the swaying motion of a rope hammock that hung on the lower side porch and that I spent hours reading in, and playing in, and fought for the possession of with my brothers.

And that periodically broke and was repaired with mismatched scrap rope and twine until there was finally more repair than hammock and the whole thing resembled something constructed by a ship-wrecked sailor.

A tall magnolia rising and falling on the other side of the banister.

I remember my father carrying me out to the car so the dogs wouldn't muddy my school dress.

I remember fallen leaves under the magnolia, big brittle glossy leaves with fuzzy undersides that we would carefully select for just the right curvature and find worms and beetles to put aboard as passengers and launch on the goldfish pond where the wind would blow them from one side to the other, and that rattled when you walked on them. I remember bright red seeds dangling on tiny filaments from the cones, and stringing them on thread to make a necklace.

I remember once a copperhead crawling into the magnolia leaves and Papa clawing at them with a rake while I held the dogs back.

The knowledge, in the back of my neck, that Maria is standing quietly in the doorway behind me. I don't turn around and she goes back to the kitchen.

More and more images. Isolated. Fragmentary.

Deciding to repair a shattered vase, and discovering that half the pieces have gone missing.

It is unclear to me now what I was hoping for, or what I am *doing* exactly.

Disburdening, maybe.

The sentence, "Overcome with emotion, she could only point."

I remember my brothers using the wisteria vine to climb to the upper porch where I lay in my bassinet. I have a clear image of the two of them, bare-chested and in shorts, pushing aside the wisteria to scramble over the railing.

They had red war paint on their faces and chests.

I asked Thornton, "Do you remember climbing the wisteria at Spring Hope?"

If that were a true memory I would not be in the picture, wearing a pink bonnet, in the bassinet.

I don't remember a bassinet otherwise.

I remember a car with the passenger door open and a single red tomato sitting on the dark brown fabric of the front seat. I have often told people that this is my earliest memory, though I actually have no idea why I think that.

Looking in the closet this morning and noticing again how many lavender and violet garments I own.

I am surprised *mysteria* is not a word.

I can stop at any point, I remind myself.

Stop writing, I mean.

Though I probably won't stop until I am too tired to go on.

Ending in that case without concluding.

Sparrows congregate on my feeder, hopping and pecking. Some fly off, others fly in, or maybe the same ones return, one sparrow resembling another exactly, unlike chickens, which except for the completely white ones are easy to tell apart.

I have a black-and-white cat that sits on the window ledge of the building across the way. It can sit there for hours. It is crazy about my sparrows.

I get other birds besides sparrows on the feeder, just ordinary town birds for the most part, cardinals, jays, chickadees, titmice, and the like, but sparrows are the most common by far.

It isn't a feeder, properly speaking, just seed spread out on a broad plank that Lester has nailed to the window ledge.

One summer we were given chickens of our own that no one was supposed to eat.

Edward told Lila he wanted to eat his chicken and he did.

Then Thornton ate his, just to show Edward.

I told them they had better not eat my chicken, but it died anyway.

Edward and Thornton tried to fly by holding an umbrella and jumping off the roof of the chicken house.

Nothing happened except they broke the umbrella.

I remember Edward throwing our cat in the goldfish pond.

The time I put my hair up in Mama's hairnet and played dress-up with Thornton, clumping around in enormous shoes and bickering like married people, and Edward said we looked stupid.

The time I hid in the dark pantry eating dog biscuits with Thornton.

The time Edward squeezed my head so hard it hurt.

The time Mama gave me a Sears and Roebuck catalog to cut up for paper dolls.

The times I was happy playing paper dolls with Thornton.

I don't remember when we stopped keeping chickens.

I remember Papa going outside to shout for Verdell and the two of them walking over to the chicken house and tearing it down.

I remember "It's cheaper to buy eggs."

Maria has moved my suitcase again. I can't imagine who she thinks is going to trip over it.

I tell her I am not going to keep Thornton waiting while I rummage in the closet trying to find my suitcase.

When Maria leaves I'll go to the closet and once again carry it back to its place by the front door.

A green nylon suitcase with wheels and a handle that pulls out for towing.

Though we never talk about the suitcase, never even say the word *suitcase,* we are engaged in a silent struggle over it.

As over my shoes, which Maria puts away the instant I take them off, unless I say to her, "Maria, please leave my shoes there," by the sofa, for example, if I have taken them off to watch television.

She doesn't like it that I write on the walls.

I remember a green station wagon with wooden sides and clusters of pale mushrooms sprouting from the wood. I remember Papa digging them out with a screwdriver and filling the cavity with putty from a little can.

I remember rolling the leftover putty into little balls and setting them on a porch railing to harden, and the smell of my hands afterwards, and how the balls crumbled to bits when I tried to play with them.

Though it might actually have been Thornton who got the leftover putty and rolled it into little balls.

I suspect a number of my early memories might actually belong to Thornton or even to Edward, and I just took them over, ingested them, so to speak, after hearing one or the other talking about them.

Though "That memory belongs to me, not you" does seem a funny thing to say.

I remember dung beetles rolling balls of dung bigger than themselves, and my mother saying they were really *scarab* beetles.

I remember learning what *metempsychosis* means.

When I recall the mushrooms sprouting from the car, the unpainted weathered wood of the house, and how rarely we received new clothes, I am amazed that as a child I was able to go for so long thinking we were wealthy.

The cat, its tail twitching, watches my sparrows, but it won't try to jump across. It knows the distance is too great and that it will fall to its death if it tries, and the sparrows know this as well and are not disturbed by the cat.

They are dumb creatures, as people say, but they know more than Edward and Thornton did when they jumped off the chicken house clutching an umbrella.

I remember the coal bin, a man-high box built right up against the side of the house back of the kitchen, with a trapdoor in the tin roof for adding coal, which is where I learned what *trapdoor* means.

I remember a big dirty coal truck, the coal men in filthy clothes standing straddle-legged on the bed, bending to the hummock of coal with wide, flat shovels, their skin a lusterless black, except on warmer days when the driver of the truck displayed rivulets of pink skin where the trickling sweat had washed it.

I remember Verdell carrying scuttles of coal in from the bin, one in each hand, Mama saying, "Hold the door for Verdell," and a scuttle standing by the fireplace in every room. I don't remember all the rooms, not from that period, when the scuttles would have stood there, though I do remember them all from later, when I wandered aimlessly in and out of them followed by dogs.

Maria has never heard the word *scuttle.*

I remember how coal tastes.

Nat King Cole came on the car radio and Mama made us all hush.

We drank water from a spigot to get the coal taste out. Thornton had black around his lips.

At some point we stopped heating with coal, and at some other point after that Papa and Verdell ripped the bin down and tossed the shattered planks, crumbling and riddled with little tunnels, into a heap in the yard. Hundreds of termites spilled out and Thornton stamped on them.

I asked Lester if he had seen my hairbrush, though he never goes in my bedroom, which is where I lost it, on the off chance. He went down and looked in the bushes in case it really did fall off the window ledge.

In portions of Africa, and other places also, I imagine, people take for granted that the spirits of the dead—their ghosts, I suppose, or their souls—linger among the living, an uncanny invisible presence that is nonetheless obvious to everyone.

It would be ridiculous of me to say that there are no ghosts just because I personally don't see them, when a great many other people do.

Maria and Lester both claim to have seen ghosts.

Failure to see them might just mean that something is wrong with me personally, that I lack the proper mental apparatus, or that my apparatus was damaged by my education.

Perhaps the same kind of apparatus Maria's mother had used to see the Virgin on a church roof.

I can't for the life of me make out what Baudelaire and Mallarmé saw in Poe, which does not mean there isn't something there.

Though that would be a different kind of apparatus, I imagine.

Or the problem might be that having become thoroughly estranged from my parents by the time they died I am estranged from their ghosts as well, who actually have lingered but are now refusing to show themselves to me out of spite.

On the other hand, if they lingered at all it would have been at Spring Hope, since it is places and especially houses that are said to be haunted, people more rarely, though I never saw them there either.

Unless Mama is in fact showing herself as best she can.

Which would be why I can't stop thinking about her.

She won't let me stop thinking about her.

I want to stop thinking about her.

Yesterday, Sunday, I was alone all day. I spent a long time making two deviled eggs for lunch. I ate one and then wasn't hungry anymore.

If I had a dog, I would have given it the other one.

I stood in the kitchen and recited Swinburne aloud. "Pale, beyond porch and portal, crowned with calm leaves she stands," and so forth.

The time I squatted next to an anthill, holding my dress up so ants couldn't climb on it, and watched Thornton soak the hill with gasoline from a mason jar and light it on fire. I have a clear image of the ants swarming out of their hole right into the flames and curling up into little black balls.

I remember chanting, "Ladybird, ladybird, fly away home, your house is on fire and your children are gone," and tossing a ladybug high in the air to make it fly.

I remember always knowing that it was wrong to kill ladybugs.

I remember "Eeny, meeny, miney, mo, catch a nigger by his toe," and my mother telling us we must say *bunny* instead.

The times I saw Lila and Mama carrying bucket-loads of clinkers from the fireplaces out to the backyard, adding them to the pile next to the wire incinerator.

The time I noticed that clinkers, tumbling one on another, went *clink.*

The time Edward and Thornton and a bunch of other boys were waging a battle with clinkers and hit my friend Lucille on the head with one, and Lila made them stop.

When Papa came home he made Edward and Thornton pick up all the clinkers from the yard and put them back on the pile.

We had oil heat by then but the clinker pile was still there. I don't remember when the pile was taken away. I do remember that for a long time no grass would grow where it had been.

Riding past the post office this morning I saw a summer tanager in a crepe myrtle. I made Lester stop and back up so I could point it out to him. He wasn't interested in seeing, but I kept pointing until he saw it.

A female summer tanager is the only greenish-yellow bird with gray-brown wings of that size found here in September, is a fact.

The image of myself on the library floor drawing birds with colored pencils, copying them from a book of Audubon paintings, is a figment.

Is a true figment, I am convinced, nonetheless.

As is the image of my mother leaning over me, inspecting my drawing.

As is the idea that my mother taught me to draw, though I have no image of that.

I do have an image of a large book called *Teach Yourself to Draw* that somebody, Edward or Thornton, had scribbled all over with green crayon, that my mother gave me to practice from.

That I was never able to draw as well as my mother is a fact.

Is an imaginary fact, of course.

James McNeill Whistler was my mother's favorite painter.

I have never seen an actual painting by Whistler.

I have never seen an actual painting by anyone famous.

I have another image of myself on the floor of the living room, but this time I am looking at illustrations of paintings in a large, thick book called *Masterpieces of the Louvre.* There is a reproduction of the *Mona Lisa* on the cover.

I remember my mother telling me it was the most famous painting in the world.

Remembering, and feeling again now, how alien and completely *bizarre* the paintings in the book were to me then.

I remember wishing I knew how to play a trumpet.

I remember sitting at the dining room table after everyone had left, the time I decided to look at a Sears and Roebuck catalog all the way through.

If you placed the telephone to your ear a female voice said, "Number, please."

I had no idea that we were small-town people.

I have gone out with Lester and bought a new hairbrush. It is made of blond wood and has natural bristles.

In addition to things I remember, there are things I only imagine that I remember, because I was told about them, perhaps, or because I made them up out of whole cloth, possibly, some of them, without even knowing it.

I have a (mental) image of Thornton standing next to an airplane, and I have another (photographic) image of the same thing on a wall in my bedroom.

I am quite sure the former is a real memory of an actual event, of Thornton standing next to an airplane when he was seventeen, and not simply a mental reflection of the photograph of a similar event.

I want to say that in the former I can feel myself there, out of view, a dozen feet from Thornton, who has completed his first flying lesson and is now posing with the airplane.

Even though I know there is no discernible difference between a real memory and a fake.

Know it theoretically, I mean.

My first word was *gun,* they told me. I believe that to be true, though I don't remember it, of course.

On the other side of the ocean there was a war going on, I know now.

I had not seen the ocean yet, though it was not far away at all.

Before actually seeing the ocean I had expected it to look the way it had in a *Little Lulu* comic strip when a huge wave rose up suddenly and knocked Tubby flat.

You could see fish swimming in the wave towering over Tubby's head before it crashed on him.

The Atlantic Ocean did not look anything like that, I found out later.

I have a lot of memories of the ocean now, accumulated over decades and decades, but none so vivid as the one where the wave knocks Tubby down.

I remember a heavy stamping of boots on the upper porch moments before soldiers, who must have climbed the wisteria to get there, burst through the French doors into my parents' bedroom.

Though I am quite certain this never happened, it remains one of the clearest of my early memories.

Edward and Thornton had stacks of war comics that I was allowed to read when I was sick, is why I have such a memory, I am sure.

German soldiers were blond, big, with handsome, cruel faces. They said "ach Himmel" when surprised and "argh" as they died.

Japanese soldiers were small, misshapen, and ugly, with large mouths and lots of big teeth. They screamed "aieeee" as they flew into the air, arms and legs akimbo, above yellow flames and the word BLAM!

I don't remember anything else about the Second World War.

I don't remember that I minded being sick.

Edward had malaria first, and then Thornton. I remember feeling proud when they told me I had malaria, finally.

I remember polio. I was not afraid, but Mama was afraid. In the end none of us got polio.

A girl in school got polio. She had one leg much shorter than the other. I didn't know her before she got polio, when her legs were the same length. Nobody was her friend.

The time Thornton and Edward dropped Crayola crayons off the upper porch onto the brick walk. The sun made them soft, and we molded them into little balls and ate them.

It must have been summer then, though I don't remember summer.

It was a long time before I could remember things like "It was summer then."

I remember how crayon tastes. Like candle.

Lila's son William was killed in the Korean War, which is all I remember about that war. I don't remember William.

In the morning quiet I can hear someone playing ping-pong in the common room.

Thornton and Edward broke the ping-pong table at Spring Hope by jumping on it.

I remember, much earlier, digging with Thornton in the dirt behind the house and finding a dented ping-pong ball, and Thornton saying it was a snake egg.

The fact that Peter Caldwell, who was Edward's friend, had a dog named Ping-Pong.

The time Edward said table tennis was the same as ping-pong.

The fact that Ping Pong was not the name of a Chinese person who invented ping-pong.

I have a single vivid memory of the French-Indochina war. From the back seat of a car I heard the words *Dien Bien Phu* issuing from a chrome grill in the dashboard. The words *fall of,* as in *the fall of Rome,* followed by that strange *unimaginable* name.

It was a black Chevrolet car, I am almost sure.

In the strangeness of the name Dien Bien Phu, in the remoteness of Indochina, lay a first dim awareness, I think now, that we were provincial people, that we lived in an out-of-the-way insignificant place.

The next war I remember was in Indochina again. The memories of that war, meaning of course the memories of the *news* of that war, are exceptionally clear, because I was an adult then and because of television, I suppose, and also quite meaningless.

If Edward had died in Vietnam someone would have told us, I am sure.

I learned to read at the same time as Thornton, who was two years older, I remember Mama telling a woman who had poked her head in through the car window.

I remember "My daughter, the genius," and my mother standing behind me, gripping my shoulders while I stared in terror at the school principal.

The time I stood at a bookcase and sounded out the names on the spines, Mama correcting me when I was wrong. "Not *Goth*, honey, it's pronounced *Gerty*."

Scolding me when I said somebody *busted* an arm or *skint* a knee but letting Edward and Thornton say them.

My father clapping his hands and saying "well, well" the time I spelled *Wednesday* after Thornton said I couldn't.

I was born knowing how to read, Mama said.

Thornton said *facetious* was not a word.

I was a naturally gifted child.

My mother's brother Louis Staunton, who went to Paris to study painting and died of a ruptured appendix before he could attend a single class, was naturally gifted.

His life was snuffed out, my mother said.

She always used the phrase *snuffed out* when speaking of the death of young artists like Louis Staunton or John Keats, whose life was snuffed out by tuberculosis.

Being snuffed out like Uncle Louis was a tragic irony, my mother said.

There was a photograph of a teenaged Louis Staunton in the library at Spring Hope. He was seated on a large white horse, a pale blond boy who looked ill, I thought.

The time I played dying with Thornton. I lay on the cracked leather sofa, beneath the picture of poor dead Louis Staunton, my hands crossed on my chest, while Thornton intoned, "She was not yet seven . . ."

There was cotton in the fields back of the house when I was very small, followed by a green bushy crop that I think now must have been soybeans, and then just tall grass that turned pale brown and grew feathery tassels in the fall, and after a time the grass also went, overtaken by shortleaf pines, which Papa called field pines, and stunted black-jack oaks.

There are houses in the fields now, I believe, but I have not gone back to look.

The soil at Spring Hope wasn't worth a goddamn, my father said.

Knowing even as a small child that we inhabited a poor, unfertile, unlucky land that nothing good would come from.

I remember my mother saying that the South was a *tragic* land.

I remember fields baking in the sun, the distant trees shimmering in the heat waves. I remember dust devils swirling across the fields.

I remember my father taking the three of us for long aimless rides in the car on hot evenings. We rolled down all the windows and tilted the vent windows to make more wind, and though the air was hot the wind made us feel cool.

Images of unpainted shacks and tumble-down sheds in small acres of poor-looking fields, mules in paddocks, hogs in makeshift slab pens, and strange dirty barefoot children my own age standing among the wandering chickens in the yards, looking up at our car, staring, unsmiling usually but sometimes waving, unsure, flow through my mind the way they flowed past the car.

I remember looking out the rear window at a cloud of dust curling behind us, and coming to a stop and the dust catching up with us and rolling over the car.

Images from different times, flowing together now.

Miles of pine forest there now, broken by roadside clearings and trailers and little brick houses without porches, and nobody outside because of air-conditioning and television, I noticed, passing in the car with Lester down the same roads, unable to attach those other images to anything there now.

Mama, Papa, Lila, Verdell are dead now. Edward too, for all I know.

I remember hot summer nights when all three of us slept on iron bedsteads that Verdell set up on the screen porch, the dogs out there with us.

The time we made music by banging on the metal bed rails with sticks and spoons as hard as we could, Papa yelling at us to stop.

The time Edward fell out of bed and then Thornton fell out of his bed on purpose, but I was afraid to fall out of mine.

I remember Mama on the porch, her back to me, working a handful of raw cotton into a torn place in the screen to stop mosquitoes getting in, immobile in that posture, in that image.

We sometimes heard, even above the continuous shrill vibrato of insects and frogs, the whistle of a freight train crossing the trestle half a mile downriver, though never the fainter clickety-clicks of the wheels, as we could sometimes in the mortuary silence of winter.

Steam locomotives, and the breathy melancholy of their whistles, were among the first things that I became aware of as having disappeared.

A steam locomotive took my mother to New York when she was young and she never forgot it.

The time I rode a train to Connecticut with Thornton and my father, taking Thornton back to college, it was a diesel locomotive.

Thornton uses an airplane to travel now.

Hearing the Cessna overhead, I would run to get Mama and rush with her into the yard and we would stand there waving.

Waving and waving while the little blue plane banked and came back over the treetops, roaring overhead, almost scraping the roof, it looked from below, the dogs frantic, leaping and barking, and the plane going away, disappearing behind the trees in the direction of the county airfield, the sound of it vanishing finally, and having scarcely time to get ready and get Mama ready before Thornton would be driving up to the house.

Showing Maria the photograph of Thornton standing by his airplane.

Maria has never flown in an airplane.

Sometimes I get Lester to take me out in the car and we just ride around.

When Lester drives me I ride in back.

When Mama or Papa drove Lila home, Lila rode in back.

The road to Lila's house went past a big sinkhole, a nearly circular pool of black water fringed with stumps of sawed-off cypress trees and a few gnarly tupelos left standing because they were trash trees not even good for burning, the grain of a tupelo log running every which way and no man alive able to split it, my father said.

If a cow went to drink in that hole and fell in, it would sink forever, Lila said.

I went to Verdell's house with my father and a goat knocked me over.

Before Lester there was Vernon, before Vernon there was Huey, and so forth.

Before Maria there was Ruth, before Ruth there was Beth, before Beth I was at Spring Hope, wandering from room to room, as I mentioned, with dogs, as I also mentioned.

It is generally true, I think, that very little of importance happens now.

I am aware of a long stretch of time, but it is mostly undifferentiated, without markers.

If I try to imagine "a long stretch of time" I picture a level landscape without trees and a narrow unpaved road running across it all the way to a distant horizon.

A long beige ribbon of time.

Even though I have never actually seen a landscape like that.

If I had to describe my situation in a word, my living situation and psychological situation, and so forth, it would be *indeterminate.*

Odd that a word like that, being quite indeterminate itself, can describe a situation so precisely.

Going on vacation with Thornton might be considered important, I suppose.

Considered important by me, naturally, though it might not be by anyone unaware of my circumstances.

The journey of the body is across physical space, on foot, horseback, bicycle, in cars, airplanes, and so forth, on foot again, stumbling, crawling at the end, metaphorically speaking.

The journey of the soul is through time. I like the odd phrase: *a space of time.* A gap between one time and another, a continuum without content, a kind of sinkhole into which weeks, months, and years have sunk from view.

I am traveling, it seems, through the space of time, falling through it actually, it feels to me now.

The body stops, but space goes on and time goes on.

The fact is I have no clear idea of what I mean by the word *soul*.

A great whoosh of feathers, and a pair of doves descends on my feeder, startling me and sending sparrows flittering off in every direction.

If a sparrow tries to come back, alighting cautiously at the very edge of the feeder, the doves puff out their chests, hunch their wings, bat-like, and strut and jut about on the feeder looking terribly frightening.

Hummingbirds, oddly, are also quite aggressive, though mockingbirds are easily the most aggressive birds I know.

Excluding hawks and falcons, of course, who are positively murderous.

Even so, birds cannot be considered neurotic.

Any bad feelings they have they get rid of by flying, I imagine.

On second thought, though, remembering now, some chickens are horribly neurotic.

And parrots, of course, as everyone knows, the ones in cages anyway, plucking out their own feathers.

As did my mother, with her hair, pulling most of it out.

I have always been crazy about birds.

Even so, I don't care for Poe.

And of course it was a crow, not a raven.

The shops had screen doors and slow-turning fans on the ceilings when I was a child.

The grocery store, the hardware, and the feed store had floors of broad wooden planks with wide cracks between them.

When you jumped on the floor of the feed store a cloud of dust came up.

The drugstore had a floor of black and white linoleum tiles. You had always to step only on black tiles or something awful would happen.

I remember Thornton, one day when he was angry at me, deliberately walking on the white tiles.

The colored man who worked in the feed store had a daughter who was born with six toes on each foot. Her father chopped the extra ones off with a kitchen knife, Mama said.

I remember Mama cutting okra at the kitchen table. She looked at my bare feet and at her knife and said, "Hmm, looks like this child's got too many toes."

I remember pretending to be frightened, and at the same time actually being a little bit frightened.

The odd phrase: "She was half pretending."

I was half frightened, I think, because I sensed that my mother was only half pretending.

We, meaning my brothers and I, liked to pretend we were orphans.

The cat sits in a patch of sunlight and washes itself. It likes pretending it doesn't care about my sparrows.

I lean across the desk, close to the open window, and wave. The cat stops washing and looks.

I remember a wizened halfwit named Doc who rode a bicycle. He was the only grown-up who rode a bicycle in that town.

The time Thornton and some other boys ran behind and pummeled him with dirt clods.

I have a clear mental image of his face, the skin of his face like creased leather, but I can't tell from the image if he was a white man or a Negro, pedaling as hard as he could.

I remember when Brazil nuts were called nigger toes.

I remember black boys swimming in Johnson Creek below the bridge, where one day we saw a very small boy with skin as white as a fish's belly.

"Look, there's an albino Negro," Edward said.

Which was how I learned the word *albino.*

Mama told us only trashy people said nigger toes.

The times Thornton fought Edward to sit in front, screaming *shotgun, shotgun,* running out the door and down the front steps, racing for the car. If Thornton reached it first Edward would drag him out, while the dogs ran around the car barking.

The time Papa grabbed Edward by the shirt collar and jerked him back so hard he fell down.

The school had tall windows that opened with cranks. Only certain boys were allowed to turn the cranks.

The car had fuzzy brown upholstery that tickled my legs if I wore shorts. We were not allowed to wear shorts at school.

The time Miss Alfa said she was going to squeeze the mush out of me in first grade, and not understanding what she meant and being frightened.

The time Thornton wouldn't let me speak to him at recess anymore, turning away and walking off, when I was in second grade.

Looking at the clock and closing my eyes and counting to a hundred and opening my eyes and looking at the clock.

I remember people asking me how I liked school, and saying "fine."

On our way to the store after school Edward stopped and yelled *phooey* and slung his books into a water-filled ditch. Then Thornton yelled *phooey* and threw his books, and then I threw mine, I believe, though I don't actually remember that part.

When we got home Papa took Edward out by the clinker pile and whipped him.

The time Edward said he wanted to be a jockey and ride racehorses, and Papa said that was a good way to end up a nobody.

The time the whole school walked to the cemetery on Confederate Memorial Day and stood among the graves and sang "Dixie" and "The Bonny Blue Flag."

The time I put Thornton's paper dolls in the fire, after he wouldn't talk to me at school.

Lester flips through *Road & Track* while he eats. When he comes across something that interests him his eyes bulge and he stops chewing in order to move his lips as he reads.

Lester is crazy about cars.

We walked to the store after school and rode home with our father. We went a long way down the same street the school was on, over the train tracks and on down that street, turned at the Presbyterian church and on down past the Amoco station, Baptist church, drugstore, movie theater, pool hall, beauty parlor, ten-cent store, ice house, furniture store, every day after school the same, walking behind Edward and Thornton.

I remember a penguin on an iceberg and the words "It's Cool Inside" on the door of the drugstore and on the ticket window at the movie theater. I remember stopping to look at movie posters. I remember a movie cost twelve cents, but I don't remember any of the posters.

The times we walked faster to get quickly past the pool hall on hot days when they had the door wide open, propped back against the wall by a dilapidated green armchair set out on the sidewalk. I remember pool tables one behind the other receding into the dim far distance, each in a cone of light cast by a metal-shaded lamp suspended above it, cigarette smoke drifting and curling in the cones, beer and tobacco smells floating out onto the sunlit sidewalk, and the hard bright clicking of the balls.

I understood that the men in the pool hall were different from us, that they came from the country or from parts of town we didn't go to, that some of them worked at the hosiery mill by the railroad tracks, but I don't know how I knew this.

We stood by the loading dock at the icehouse and waited for them to open the door and drag out a big block of ice, and when the wave of cold air hit us we opened our mouths and said "aaah."

I remember "Let's wreck the train," the time Thornton and Floyd Denton put trash on the railroad tracks, hauling bricks, rocks, a rotten log with ants in it, I remember in particular, and piling them all on a rail.

The time I put a dime on a rail and couldn't find it afterwards, looking everywhere in the rock ballast between the ties and in the grass next to the tracks, Thornton saying I was stupid to put a dime.

We stood by the tracks and waved to the people in the windows flashing past.

The time a girl about my own age looked out a window at me, and then, turning her head, continued looking even as the train was rushing her away.

Imagine looking from the window of a speeding train at a child in a short summer dress standing by the tracks on the outskirts of a small Southern town, a tiny white figure against a hill of rampant kudzu dwindling in the distance as the train speeds northward even as you continue to look, pressing your cheek against the window glass, until she has entirely vanished.

Remembering it now in just that way, as if I were the one on the train, waving good-bye to myself.

When Edward was older he came home on his own, and later still Edward and Thornton had cars. I was not going to school anymore by the time they had cars.

Edward's car was a black Ford. I sat inside while he washed it and then rinsed it off with the garden hose. I put my face against the window and he shot spray at it.

I remember knowing Fords were better than Chevrolets.

I don't remember what kind of car Thornton had.

I remember waking up on the backseat of Thornton's car when Papa shone a flashlight through the side window, the time I ran away.

Edward and Thornton were crazy about cars.

Edward went away in his car, spinning the wheels and throwing up dirt and gravel.

I have an image of my father standing on the front steps in a hat, coat, and tie. I want to say that he is watching Edward go.

Last night I turned off all the lights and sat in a chair by the living room window to watch a lunar eclipse, more keyed up than I have been in a long time, not agitated, though, just happy to be caught up in waiting for something other than meals, walks, death I suppose, and Thornton, in this case just a lunar eclipse, and so wasn't as burdened as usual, when I fell asleep and missed it.

I find myself thinking, "What in the world will I write next?" pronouncing the words in my head, because that is what my mother was always saying, sitting at this desk also.

Even though I am not at a loss for words.

Unlike her, who would grab her hair at the temples and pull at it and rock side to side, saying, "It won't come, why won't it come?" or look up at the ceiling and say, "Make it come, Lord, please make it come," and other such histrionics, after she was the way she would eventually become, sadly.

I can't imagine what it was like to be my mother.

I am not a writer, is the problem.

One can't put everything into words.

Maria reaches in and closes the door to my room. Even with it closed I can hear her vacuuming in the hall, the vacuum cleaner knocking against the baseboards.

Maybe I'll get Thornton to rent me a cottage at the beach, one with a screen porch overlooking the ocean, where I can sit and listen to the surf and the seabirds and be completely alone, even if that means keeping house and making meals for myself. I can get a dog. I would rather have a dog than Maria, I will tell him.

I am shutting windows, doors, pulling down blinds, shrinking into the cupboard of the self, I understand that.

The sentence, "She wanted to be alone with herself."

Wanting for a little while at least to be alone without myself.

Wanting to save my mother from drowning, when I can't stay afloat myself, clinging to this inventory of tiny things.

The times we rode the bus to school, on fall mornings when Papa took Verdell and went hunting or when he drove the truck to High Point to buy furniture.

I remember "The least he could do is leave me Verdell."

The time I touched my forehead to the bus window and recoiled when it made my head vibrate, and doing it again on purpose.

The time I looked out the bus window and saw a pig hanging by its hind legs from a tree limb, strung up like that so they could bleed it, Edward said.

I remember the fascination of the pig, the mingling of horror and attraction engendered by the image of the pig. I remember Mama hushing me when I tried to talk about the pig.

I remember Thornton drawing in crayon a picture of the pig and writing at the bottom, "The Death of the Pig."

I remember, later, a photo of Mussolini and his mistress strung up like that.

I remember always knowing that we were superior to other families of our acquaintance.

I thought of us vaguely as "illustrious."

Yesterday after breakfast I lay on the sofa with my eyes closed. Even from there, in the Sunday quiet, I could hear sparrows on the windowsill, chirping. I could hear the ruffled flutter of their wings as they came and went, and the faint *tick tick* of their beaks on the feeder.

Maria has found my brush under the sofa, covered with dust and what looks like dog hair, though of course it is not dog hair.

The time I was walking to the store from school and saw Thornton fighting on the ground with another boy, the other boy sitting on his chest, and some older boys in a ring around them shouting and laughing, and Edward was there, leaning in, yelling pointers to Thornton, urging him to *buck* the other boy off.

When Thornton saw me he started crying and the other boy got off his chest and Edward turned and walked away. I couldn't see his face. He walked with his arms crooked and rigid and his shoulders hunched, because he was ashamed of Thornton, I could tell.

The time Edward and Thornton were fighting each other and Mama screamed at them to stop, and Edward stopped and Thornton hit him in the mouth.

The time we climbed out of Edward's bedroom window and sat on the porch roof, Thornton and Edward smoking cigarettes one after another. Thornton got up and walked to the edge and looked down. "Dropping a brick from up here would be a good way to kill somebody," he said.

The time Edward hit Thornton in the face with a tree branch and almost put out his eye, Mama said.

The time Thornton dropped a metal trash can loaded with bricks down the stairwell hoping to hit Edward who was talking on the phone in the hall below and missed by a mile but splintered a floorboard.

Rummaging in a drawer for my yellow socks, not finding them, and sitting on the bed while Maria looks in the drawer. When she fails to find them, she sits down on the bed beside me, and we wonder aloud about the socks.

Going past the pool hall with Thornton one day when the door was open and we couldn't help seeing inside, we saw several men bunched around a table near the door. A tall bald man we recognized from the feed store was leaning across it, elbow drawn back, preparing to shoot, and standing opposite him, holding a cue stick, was Edward. He turned his head and looked, and nothing in his face revealed that he knew us. I have a clear image of how he looked at that moment. His hair was slicked back and he looked mean and furtive.

The time Thornton and Edward stood in the yard and shot at cans with a pistol, and Mama told them to go away from the house if they were going to shoot, and they went out on the dike and threw tin cans and bottles in the water and shot at those.

They shot at a bullfrog. The bullets splashed around it and it disappeared, and on the way back we saw it floating upside down. They tried to reach it with a cattail but it was too far out and the cattail broke.

Edward held my hand and I shot at it.

First the brush, now the socks.

I remember walking down the highway to Dillard's Esso, which was the only place except coloreds' houses close enough to go to on foot from Spring Hope, walking on the pavement if we were barefoot, because of sandspurs in the grass, and stepping off it when we heard a car, unless the pavement was too hot to walk on, then walking cautiously in the grass anyway.

Sitting on the pavement crying and covering my foot with my hands to stop Edward from pulling a sandspur out, the time he walked off and left me.

The times we hitched rides to Dillard's on a buckboard, dangling our legs off the back, the mule clip-clopping no faster than we could have walked.

Mary-Jo Dillard was Edward's girlfriend the whole time he was in high school, and sometimes she came out to pump gas in our car instead of Mr. Dillard. I have a clear image, almost photographic, of pretty blonde Mary-Jo smiling at me through the rear window of the car.

I was crazy about Mary-Jo Dillard.

The time I was ashamed after I told Edward that Mary-Jo Dillard had pumped gas in our car and he just shrugged.

I remember thinking the Civil War was fought between North Carolina and South Carolina, and when I found out otherwise, being happy I hadn't actually said that to anyone.

I was embarrassed the time in school when I didn't know what my father did for a living.

I was embarrassed the time my mother came to school and read her poems.

I was embarrassed when, after stealing a Snickers bar from the drugstore, the lady found it in my pocket.

The time my mother bought a toy army tank for Thornton's birthday, and when the salesgirl handed her the package my mother said "Tank you," and I was embarrassed.

I remember standing at the tall mirror in my room and being embarrassed by the way I looked, wishing my arms and legs were fatter.

I wished I looked like Maureen O'Hara.

I liked the word *buxom.*

I remember hating the way my pale skin became red and splotchy when I was overheated or flustered or when I cried.

I disliked the word *pasty.*

I remember "Eve Taggart looks like a maggot," at school.

I remember standing at the mirror and watching myself scream.

I wasn't homely, I was plain. I had a beautiful soul, Mama said. Now I probably have no soul at all, though the word *soul* remains weirdly resonant.

Like the word *home*.

Thinking about that now, standing in the doorway to my bedroom, looking at the bed, the little pine table by the bed, the dresser, the bookcase, the two windows, the air conditioner, the framed photographs on the bookcase, and saying the word *home* to myself, then pronouncing it out loud several times, as an experiment, and being reminded of the expression "The words rang hollow."

If I had had a child it would have been different, I suppose.

And Thornton too without children, so it will end with us, probably.

Which is for the best. I don't see that we represent anything anymore.

Images like pictures, frozen like snapshots mostly, but memories of sounds as well. The ability to hear them again in the silence of thought somehow.

The sound of my father's whistle when he came through the door after work, four notes, two high, two low, and my mother's answering whistle, softer, higher, hearing it in my head now and noticing how it resembles the song of a chickadee. I can't imagine my father intended it that way, though my mother, who could imitate dozens of bird songs, might have.

Followed by the sound of ice in highball glasses, and a (mental) picture of them side by side on the sofa in the library, my mother lighting a cigarette, and then lighting a second cigarette by holding it to the smoldering tip of the first and handing that one to my father. I remember them sitting there smoking and rattling the ice in their glasses.

That was when I was quite small, I am sure. I don't remember when they stopped having drinks in the evening together or when my father began to come through the door without whistling.

They must have stopped before I could arrange events on a timeline, so to call it, with things starting up and going on for a while and then ceasing at definite points.

Looking at the image I have of them seated side by side in the library, hearing the murmur of their conversation from outside in the hall and the peaceful clinking of the ice, I can see they were happy together.

I remember a buzzer sounding at the rear of Taggart's Home Furnishings when someone pushed through the front door. I remember wiggling the door back and forth to make the buzzer go on and off and Papa's angry voice coming from the little room at the far back of the store that he called his office, where he dwelled by day, seated amid the disordered passel of his law books, his business plans, his stocks, his deeds, at a colossal desk beneath the framed photographs of his father and grandfather, who had each striven more or less honestly to turn a dollar into a dollar-five and had each in the long run become more or less prosperous before losing it all and so forcing the next generation to start again from scratch, to emulate what it could not inherit, I was told many times over the years, our father reciting bitterly.

I remember important papers that were not to be fiddled with, a cut-glass ashtray the size of a dinner plate, wet cigar and cigarette butts, a black iron safe on the floor, its ornate gold writing worn nearly away. I remember shelves stacked with business papers tied up in bundles with blue and red ribbons, a row of empty Coke bottles on a windowsill, dead insects among the bottles, a swivel chair that squeaked if you leaned back in it, and how we took turns spinning in the chair.

The time Edward put a cigar butt between his teeth and pretended to write checks. When Thornton tried to pull the cigar out of his mouth, he wouldn't let go. The cigar broke and Edward spit and little bits of wet cigar flew all over my dress.

I don't remember what happened after that. Edward was punished, I suppose, but I don't remember that either.

I do remember that my father smoked cigars at the store and on the porch at home and smoked Chesterfield cigarettes inside the house.

An image of my father arriving in the dining room clasping an extinguished stub of cigar between

thumb and forefinger and placing it on the edge
of his plate.

I remember the time Edward said he wouldn't
mind if communists killed Papa.

Why do I remember some things and not others?

The fact that Mallarmé holds a cigar in his hand in
Manet's portrait of him, for example.

The fact that Thornton's bicycle was red. That Sid-
ney Wilson's pony was named Trigger. That the
man who owned the pawnshop was a Jew. That
the woman named Ma Cree who walked around
town with a croker sack of old clothes was a witch.
That there were girlie magazines under the board
games in Edward's bottom drawer. That my dolls
were named Clementine, Hephzibah, and Jane-
Esmeralda. That my mother named them that.
That Clementine would only close one eye when

I laid her down. That Thornton called his bicycle the Red Hornet. That Edward could say the Lord's Prayer in Pig Latin. That he knew sixteen cuss words. That Mr. Belton who ran the jewelry store had a father who had shot himself. That horses sweat but people perspire.

The times I went to the store and my father's friends were there. They sat on the furniture that was for sale and drank whiskey from dirty glasses. They talked and joked and told hunting stories and gossiped about money and business deals, and the words flew over my head and I paid them no more attention than I did the sound of traffic outside.

The time I saw Mr. Tiller, who was a lawyer, asleep on a sofa, his mouth open, breathing noisily like a walrus, and I was embarrassed for him.

The times I sat with Mr. Colvin in one of the big armchairs. I remember the smell of bay rum and the thick black hair that curled out of the V in his shirt and more black hair on the backs of his hands.

The time he showed Edward how to blow smoke rings and then let Thornton try, but Thornton hadn't learned how to smoke yet and had a fit of coughing and ran outside.

I remember very tall Mr. Truesdale bending way over and placing his hands on his knees when he talked to me. He had bushy eyebrows and a cloudy walleye and I remember not liking him so close.

The time I asked Mr. Truesdale what he had in his pocket and he said it was a little nigger boy.

The image I have of my father from that time is of a short stocky man in a brown woolen waistcoat. He always wore woolen waistcoats in winter, I am convinced, though none of my other images include a waistcoat of any sort.

A short twisted wound-up man stuffed with coiled springs that were always about to fly loose, I suppose I can say, though I don't know that from the image.

*Wiry* is how people would have thought of him then, I imagine.

Obsessed with deals, with making money by his wits, by being smarter than the next guy, is an opinion I formed at some point.

His people were all that way, Mama said. *Mercenary* was her word for it.

He smoked constantly and cursed under his breath each time he burned a hole in a waistcoat. Rancor ate his heart.

I could not have known that then.

I have a memory, from much later, of Papa and Edward talking at the kitchen table, gossiping about deals, marveling at big deals or clever deals, where somebody was a big winner or a big loser, and my mother saying that those two brought out the worst in each other.

The time I stood in the field back of the house, the tall brown grass white and stiff with frost, and Papa said "Give me your hands" and rubbed them roughly between his two hands, hurting.

They were big hands for a man his size, with square palms and short, thick fingers, I remember noticing one day, seeing them on the steering wheel.

My mother explaining that they were peasant hands, saying that everyone in Papa's family had hands like that, and feet as well. "Wide stump-toed feet with fallen arches, amphibian hands and feet, suited for crawling on soft earth and mud, instruments designed for digging and pawing," she said much later in front of everyone, pacing and fulminating.

Reciting something she had written out beforehand, we could tell, the times she spoke like that.

I remember always knowing that Mama's people were superior to Papa's people.

I remember her taking care to pronounce the *o* in "Negro."

The woman in Nina's House of Beauty where Mama had her hair done said it was a crying shame I hadn't taken piano, and Mama said, "Well she does have an artist's hands," and held up her own hands as proof.

An image of my mother and her sister Alice painting their nails on the porch at Spring Hope while I sit in a rocking chair watching. I am wearing white lace-up shoes, and my feet don't extend past the edge of the chair. Aunt Alice reaches over to push the rocking chair with a freshly painted hand, her fingers splayed wide, using only the heel of her hand against the back of the chair so as not to smudge her nails.

I remember, another time, sitting at Mama's dresser painting my nails. When I showed her she laughed and took the polish off with cotton and polish remover and repainted them neatly.

I remember liking the way nail polish smelled.

I have a mental picture of my mother at the desk writing, the very desk I am seated at now, can see her there (here) bent over a notebook, filling a page with jagged blue script. I can see the shapes of the letters, which are angular, nearly cuneiform, as if constructed of tiny matchsticks, but I can't make out a single word, perhaps because the picture belongs to a time before I could read.

She has a cigarette in her other hand, forgotten in her intense concentration, the column of ash lengthening and falling off.

I am tempted to say that I remember my mother at her *escritoire.*

I can't bear the thought that her life might have been different.

I remember "Get out and walk through the door or be dragged there," the day I refused to go to school and my father dragged me across the schoolyard.

I remember sitting on a curb, using the hem of my dress to pat the blood off my knee after being dragged, and a colored lady in a big yellow hat bending over me, calling me honeychild.

I remember standing on the kitchen steps and looking out across an overgrown field toward the river glittering and flashing through the winter trees, the sun shining brighter than ever before, the time I was so happy after my mother promised I wouldn't have to go to school ever again.

I remember "She knows more than her teachers."

"What you want is to raise her up a misfit," my father saying.

I remember liking the word *misfit.*

The times, once a month, that my mother or Edward drove me to Columbia so I could take books out of the university library.

"She is the only person her age allowed to take books out of that library," my mother saying proudly.

I remember riding down Bull Street and looking out the car window at the long gray wall of the State Asylum, and being aware that there were crazy people on the other side.

Reading poems by Baudelaire and Mallarmé with my mother, looking up the words we didn't know and writing the English meaning in pencil above the French.

The time we resolved to speak only French together but then had to give it up when we couldn't agree on how to pronounce it.

French would have been useful, if I had learned it better, had I traveled to foreign countries, as I never doubted when I was small that I would someday, as I am sure I really might have, otherwise.

I first saw the word *verdâtre* in a poem by Baudelaire.

Whistler's painting of his mother hung on the bedroom wall above the blanket chest we sat on while trying to read poems by Mallarmé, who just happened to be a close friend of Whistler's, as I mentioned.

A coincidence that makes me want to say something like everything is connected, things hang together, and so forth.

Though I firmly believe that everything is flying apart. Or falling apart. Deteriorating generally.

Though not everywhere equally, or not everywhere obviously.

It sounds funny to say that the little children I see playing in the park are deteriorating, though of course they are actually, if you think about it, deteriorating behind the scenes, so to speak, unbeknownst even to themselves, luckily.

The worm of death is at them, and so forth.

The names Mallarmé, Whistler, Monet, and the rest are left over from when I was a genius.

Passenger pigeons, flight after flight "in countless multitudes" so dense they dimmed the sun, passed overhead continuously for three days, according to Audubon.

The last Carolina parakeet died in the Cincinnati Zoo in the same cage the last passenger pigeon had died in four years earlier, I learned recently, speaking of coincidences.

*National Geographic* magazine is the saddest thing I have ever read.

An increasingly large portion of my mind is occupied with grim statistics, I have noticed lately.

The fact that 150 million feral and free-ranging domestic cats kill two billion birds every year in the United States, while 100 million or so die in collisions with the window glass of buildings, and so forth, for example.

They see the sky reflected in the glass and fly into it.

You don't come across all those dead birds at once, of course, in a stack, or all those cats, and that makes it hard to visualize the actual numbers, the 150 million hissing, snarling cats and their mountain of dead birds, Dead Bird Mountain not being a feature on the landscape of Earth.

It is a feature on the landscape of the Planet Dearth, which is a feature on the landscape of my mind.

D standing for Devoid, Desolate, Dying, D is for Demented, and the low Depressing Drone the planet makes. People on the moon can hear it, I imagine.

A few hundred snow leopards remaining, and so forth.

Ivory-billed woodpeckers, passenger pigeons, Carolina parakeets, as I mentioned, just to name ones I might actually have seen otherwise, are gone.

Buffalo gone, prairie  gone, swamps drained or flooded, coastal marsh vanishing, the elms at Spring Hope dead, chestnuts dead almost everywhere.

Sometimes, waking up on the Planet Dearth, I can still glimpse, blue and beautiful, the true Earth, the planet of Eden, unreachable, infinitely lovely, lost, plunging through space, unguided, blind.

My mind, I want to say, is like a cage full of dead birds.

The time when I was six and somebody spotted a bear in the river swamp, the first bear sighted there in thirty years. Businesses closed all over town so men could go hunt the bear. Papa took us down to where they had laid it out on a concrete slab back of the Amoco station. The fur, streaked with brown mud, was wet and cold when we touched it. They hosed it off at the station and the water ran pink into the street. They propped its mouth open with a stick, and we reached in and touched the teeth.

Mama was crazy about birds.

Chickadees are the least aggressive birds I know.

Along with their magazine the National Audubon Society sends me invitations to travel to places all over the world, even to the Amazon Jungle, with other members to look at birds.

There were more birds, more different kinds of birds, at Spring Hope than there are here.

Waterbirds—egrets, herons, gallinules, kingfishers, rails, ospreys, anhingas, grebes, and the like, ducks of all sorts.

And forest and field birds—owls, hawks, kites, quail, shrikes, cuckoos, killdeer, woodpeckers, whip-poor-wills, and so forth.

Warblers, finches, fly-catchers, thrushes, kinglets, nuthatches, tanagers, towhees, mockingbirds, thrashers, catbirds, vireos, always in the trees and bushes around the house.

Cedar waxwings and blackbirds arrived in great swirling flocks in the fall, crows and grackles thronged the treetops and strutted in the fields.

The many times pileated woodpeckers hammered at the house, digging for grubs of carpenter bees, ripping big pieces from the siding and excavating fist-sized holes in the fascias and the tops of the columns, Verdell or one of my brothers going outside to shout and clap their hands or throw sticks to drive them off.

The bees themselves drilling neat little bullet-sized holes, buzzing furiously, while sending a steady stream of sawdust down past the windows.

The time Mama, looking out the window at a little drizzle of dust, said that one day there would be more hole than house.

I remember strangers showing up at Spring Hope, asking permission to look at birds, and walking out on the dikes with telescopes and cameras, even in December, in cold rain, or in September, in clouds of mosquitoes.

Papa going out to greet them and standing awhile talking, informative, gracious. *Seigniorial* is how he looked to me then, I think now.

Sitting in the kitchen talking to Maria about the birds at Spring Hope, not talking to her actually in a conversational way, just listing the different kinds of birds I remember there, and being aware that I am boring her silly but going on anyway, while Lester cleans under his fingernails with a tine of his breakfast fork, his eyes puckered.

The realization that I have become a tiresome old person.

The time Verdell built a whole stack of bird feeders out of wood from the chicken house and set them out in a row on the back steps, Mama coming down to look, and later he mounted them on creosote posts that he planted around the yard in such a way that standing at any window in the house we could look out and see birds, and every year or so putting up new ones to replace those that had rotted away.

I remember liking the way creosote smelled. Telephone poles, railroad tracks, and the bridge over Johnson Creek smelled of creosote on the hot days of summer.

If I close my eyes and think of summer, a variety of sounds, pictures, flavors even, floats into consciousness, but I don't smell anything except creosote and dust.

I have an image of my mother as viewed from the back, standing at a window with raised binoculars.

And another of her making the rounds of the feeders, adding seed from a metal pail.

The time sleet was ticking at the windowpanes and Mama was outside in Papa's big canvas jacket.

The time she chased Thornton around the house trying to put her ice-cold hands down his shirt.

Later, when age and illness had accentuated the sharp nose and long delicate neck, she came to look like a bird. Sitting in church with her shoulders hunched up, she looked like a stork.

A cold rainy morning and we were still at breakfast, the time Papa and Verdell came in carrying a bushel basket between them, the dogs pushing through the door behind them, and laid the ducks out on newspaper spread open on the kitchen floor. Papa quizzing the boys, poking each duck in turn with the toe of his boot, drilling them on the names, and hushing me when I tried to answer.

Canvasback. Pintail. Teal. Mallard. Lila shooed the dogs out.

I remember my mother and Lila plucking ducks at a table in the yard, plucking chickens, plucking quail. I remember Lila working smoothly, steadily, with strong big-knuckled hands, and the angry way Mama jerked at the feathers and the tearing sound of the feathers coming off. They fished out livers and hearts with bloody hands and tossed the rest of the innards to the dogs.

I sat between them and when the down feathers went in my nose I snorted to get them out and Mama said to use a Kleenex.

I remember the dogs at Spring Hope, gun dogs mainly, English setters and springer spaniels for the most part.

I can recall the names of most and maybe even all of the dogs we owned over the years but the names of only three of my classmates.

Dana, Alex, Joseph, Henry, Big Boy, Bosco, Lucy, Beau, Venus, Rusty, Laddie, Cluny, Kirk, and so forth, were dogs.

The time Venus bit Jimmy Watts. No one liked Jimmy Watts, and we were all glad when Venus bit him, except Mama, who had to drive Jimmy home and apologize.

The fact that Mama's little dog Margaret ate sugar lumps, was given scraps at the table, and became almost too fat to walk.

The fact that Margaret was afraid of Papa and sat between Mama's feet when he was in the room.

I remember crying when Mr. Tully, who brought us firewood, ran over Lucy with his truck. Thornton said you could see her insides.

How Margaret just vanished, killed by a coon or an alligator probably, Papa said, nodding in the direction of the river.

I told people at school that an alligator ate my dog.

I remember the stray dogs that crept in from the highway, mangy, cowering, half-starved curs that Papa called coloreds' dogs, that slunk under the kitchen porch, where we would find them curled up in the dirt and lure them out with food.

That disappeared after a day or two, Mama saying they had run off, when actually Papa or Verdell took them out to the woods and shot them, I found out later.

At the desk writing, and becoming aware that I am talking to myself, reciting the names of dogs.

At my bedroom window last night, preparing to pull the shade, I looked out at the rain and saw Thornton standing in a doorway on the other side of the passage—Thornton the way he was then, I mean, not Thornton the man of today—but it was another little boy, obviously.

I have an image of Thornton stretched out on his back on the rug in my room, hands clasped behind his head, eyes wide open, fixed on the ceiling, and of me in the bed next to Mama, while she read to us from *Peter Pan.*

The many times, later, that we played Peter Pan and Wendy.

Peter Pan and Wendy consisting mostly of walking around in the yard while Thornton made up adventures and told them to me.

We were brother and sister in the stories.

Edward wouldn't play.

Afterwards, while Thornton was in school, I wrote the adventures down in a book Mama made by sewing sheets of stationery together with shoelaces. We made drawings for the book and drew colored maps of all the places we had been in the stories.

I remember holding Thornton's hand and flying over the roof of the chicken house.

I remember "That's mine," and Edward balling the tarp up in his arms. Without the tarp we were left sitting in bright sunlight with our plates and spoons.

The book was called *Peter Pan and Wendy at Spring Hope.*

It was a book about orphans.

Thornton scribbled all over some of the pages of the book after Mama said *facetious* was a word.

I went on writing adventures in the book even after he stopped playing.

Babies were birds before they were humans, and small children can still remember the bird-stage if they try hard, in *Peter Pan*.

The time Thornton took me up in an actual airplane and we flew down the coast. We flew low over the beach, and people in bathing suits looked up and waved.

We were not pretending to fly then. We were actually flying while pretending to be ordinary people.

Chagall was my favorite painter. He painted pictures of people flying through the air.

Even as a child I was crazy about Thornton.

The time my mother, rising abruptly from the table, said to my father, "We are *not* ordinary people."

The many times I sat with Thornton on the black leather sofa in the library while Mama read poetry out loud.

The sofa cushions were split and oozed cotton stuffing. The time I tried to push it back in and Mama said I was just making it worse.

In my memories of Mama reading it is always raining outside.

Droplets trickled down the windowpanes, and she switched on the lamp behind her chair.

She read "The Rime of the Ancient Mariner," "Childe Harold," "Ode to the West Wind," "Dover Beach," "The Lady of Shalott," "How They Brought the Good News from Ghent to Aix," "Annabel Lee," and so forth, when we were still quite small.

My mother was fond of Poe.

Sometimes, reading, she was overcome by beauty and cried.

She couldn't read Edna St. Vincent Millay or Keats without crying.

Sometimes I think she was driven crazy by beauty.

Mama, moved by a book or poem, would say that it was *devastating*. *Tess of the D'Urbervilles* was completely devastating, I remember.

Looking for Mama is in some ways like being lost in a dense forest, as I said earlier, and in some other ways it is like being lost in a thick fog or in a desert, as I also said.

Though I have never actually been lost in any of those places, I do have a precise image of being lost in a forest, one that I invented as a child while Mama was reading me the story of Hansel and Gretel.

I remember, from my mother then, stories drawn from the lives of artists. She told us about Robert Browning eloping to Italy with Elizabeth Barrett, that Shelley went sailing in a storm in a boat named Ariel and drowned, that Poe had a cat called Catarina, and so forth.

I don't actually remember her recounting any of those stories, don't possess, I mean, a little internal movie that shows her telling them to me. But in the case of certain facts, so to call them, like the ones mentioned above, it seems to me there was never a moment that I didn't know them.

Unlike the story of Gérard de Nerval and the pet lobster he leashed with a blue ribbon and took for strolls in the garden of the Palais Royal, supposedly, which I do remember my mother recounting brightly at the supper table one night, having just read it somewhere, I imagine.

I remember my father saying that Gérard de Nerval sounded like an idiot.

Artists, according to Mama, were frequently eccentric, odd behavior being a natural consequence of genius.

She would have liked to be eccentric herself, I understood later, but didn't dare because of Papa and the children and her position in the town and because in fact she hated being the subject of gossip.

More eccentric than she actually was, I mean, beyond the lavender dresses.

I inherited from her the idea that an artist has to be extravagant, even though she was never able to become truly extravagant herself.

Even though I am not myself an artist.

I almost wrote the *fatal* idea that an artist, etc., which is what it was for her in a sense.

I don't remember Mama saying, "Modigliani was a debauched lunatic," but I am convinced she did say that.

*Lunatic* was one of the words she applied to extravagant artists she admired. She used the term, I want to say, fondly.

She also used the word *immortal* without irony. I have never met anyone else who could do that.

A provincial woman who never learned to be cynical.

"Your mother's a funny bird," my father said.

The time she said to my father, "I won't have illiterate children."

The time she took Thornton and me to Columbia to view an exhibit of Blake's drawings, and Thornton was bored. He sat in back on the way home and kicked the front seat even after Mama told him he had better stop. She said, "Just keep that up and I'll tell your father."

I was aware that superior people must not be bored by art.

I remember always knowing that Edward was not artistic.

The time, much later, that I tried to visit an art museum in order to see real paintings, the time I was in Connecticut with Thornton.

I remember walking there with him, crossing the campus when the carillon in the tower started ringing and students in coats and ties were suddenly all around us on the sidewalk. I was the only girl and Thornton wouldn't let me take his arm. He said to everyone we met, "This is my kid sister."

I remember that I cried when we found out the museum was closed to the public, sensing, I suppose, even then, that I was never going to see an actual painting by anyone famous.

Standing out front to watch the people who had invitations climb out of taxis and go in through the door, some in evening wear, though it was the middle of the afternoon, and thinking that these flat, bland, ordinary-looking men and women were the very ones Mama meant when she talked about cultured people and people of sophisticated taste, and Thornton remarking that they were *swank*.

Realizing later that she had invented a whole society of people that didn't exist anywhere, one composed exclusively of people like the Brownings and

Keats and Whistler and so forth, who in addition to being geniuses were kind and generous and helpful to each other, though she would never have admitted that even to herself.

An image of my mother kneeling in the upstairs hall, putting a notebook away in a tall mahogany secretary that stood just outside the door to her bedroom, pressing down on the stack of notebooks with the palm of one hand while pushing the drawer shut with the other, frozen in that posture, in that image.

I remember always knowing that the notebooks were important.

Other drawers of the secretary held linen from my grandmother that we never used and that fell apart in our hands when we took it out later, like the past, it occurs to me now, locked away in all the little drawers, opening them now and finding it has crumbled away.

She wrote in ordinary composition books, the kind with marbled black-and-white covers that one sees everywhere still, with a white rectangle in the center of the front cover and lines for name and subject. On the line for name she put a number. I don't remember any of the numbers. I don't know how many notebooks there were.

I remember "Please don't lean on me like that," the times I stood next to her while she was writing in a notebook.

If I shut my eyes, I can turn my head in the image, so to speak, and look at a page covered with her script. Despite being able to do that, or imagine that I am doing that, I can't make out any of the words that are on it. The image of the page within the larger image of my mother seated at her desk is blurred like a photograph that is too small or too out of focus. If I stare at it, so to speak, it wavers as if glimpsed through water.

I want to say that the page has drowned in the river of time.

I sometimes imagine, absurdly, that if I could recollect some moment in the past with sufficient intensity, I would be able to live it again exactly as before.

Peter Pan wasn't able to remember anything for very long because he was never going to die.

Not that he wasn't *able* to remember exactly, it was just that he needn't bother, I think, needn't grasp at such meager immortality when an eternity of new experiences lay before him.

Ahead of me, I want to say now, I have only the past.

A truly crazy attempt to make time flow backwards.

I remember Mama reading her poems to Thornton and me, and later just to me, reading from a notebook that she held at eye level in front of her, like a schoolgirl, I thought even then.

Reciting above the hiss of rain that, it seems now, always accompanied her readings, as I mentioned earlier.

Not caring that we grasped almost nothing, apparently.

Is the reason, I suppose, that I can't remember any words.

The fact that with my eyes closed I can see her reading, on the sofa in the library, usually, or at her desk or on the bed in her room, but all I hear is rain.

The fact that she mailed her poems and stories to magazines and reviews that always mailed them back, until she finally found a few small enough and obscure enough to print them. A newspaper in Charleston sometimes printed one of her poems.

I was fifteen when I finally understood that my mother's poems were not literature.

I felt like a murderer.

If I had learned that my father was a molester of children, that would have been easier to accept than that my mother's poems were not literature.

I understood that regardless of what had happened and might still happen to her externally, her life within had come to nothing.

The many times I looked out the window at my mother on the rope swing in the yard, scarcely moving the swing, staring at the ground in front of her.

"Is she going to spend the rest of her life on that swing?" my father said.

The time she saw Rimbaud standing in the cotton.

The time she fell to her knees in the church aisle and my father and my aunt Alice took her out, and after that she wouldn't go to church anymore.

The hours and days she lay on the library sofa with her eyes closed.

I remember "I don't want God to see me."

Behind the locked door of the library, writing and balling up pages, starting a new sheet in an attempt to record her failure on the previous sheet, and giving up and stopping, forever she would say, and then starting again, hopeful once more, Thornton driving to town to buy her more paper when my father wouldn't.

I remember "I have become dust."

Wandering the house, agitated, her hair every which way, wringing her hands, wild-eyed, like a crazy person, binoculars dangling from her neck.

My mother was the only person I have ever known who actually wrung her hands, grasping the fingers of one hand in the fist of the other and twisting and squeezing, exactly as one would twist and squeeze a washcloth.

The time my father told us she was just pretending.

Thinking even then that she was just half-pretending.

Wanting to get my attention, Maria opens the door softly, stands in the doorway behind me, and shuffles her feet.

The time I was standing in my room playing *Tristan and Isolde* as loud as I could make the little record player go, when my father came up behind me and touched me on the shoulder and I was so startled I fell down.

The fact that Mama hated people coming up behind her while she was at her desk, locked the door to the library so people couldn't startle her by coming up and touching her while she was writing.

The year I let my hair tangle and wouldn't bathe or change my clothes, when I was always listening to *Tristan and Isolde,* when I was fourteen or fifteen, was the time my mother was locked in the library.

My most vivid memory from that time is of the voice of Kirsten Flagstad.

It was a portable record player in a hard case that would close up and lock. It had a handle on top and when shut looked like a piece of Samsonite luggage.

I used Mama's Samsonite suitcase to travel to Connecticut later, the time I rode the train with Thornton and my father.

Ordinary things—luggage, radios, toasters, and so forth—looked just the way things were then. Similar items today look just the way things are now. I can't explain this.

Memories also. It is impossible, I think, for anyone to have memories like mine now.

She dwelled in the wreckage of her poems, sat in the house in one or another of her lavender dresses and fantasized about a life that fate, my father, and the South had denied her but that she could not let go of, that she mourned the loss of, while the only real life she possessed slipped past her almost unobserved, her husband and children grew away from her, became actually frightened of her.

As if a foreign body had invaded the family. It could not be expelled, so we isolated it within the system, gave her wide berth when we passed her in the kitchen or hall and avoided looking directly at her, into her eyes, as if the system had formed a protective cyst around her.

I want to say that the foreign body was my mother's soul, dwelling among us like a spirit of the dead, not resting, not able to find any peace, wandering the house, distraught.

If only I knew what I meant by *soul*.

The world seems to me such a poor and barren place, I can't imagine what a soul would find to live on here.

The times she came into a room and the conversation faded and then resumed as a pretend conversation, stiff or animated in a false way, sounding rehearsed and wooden.

We were puppets, my mother said. We were little wooden dolls. She said she could see the strings.

I remember "Why don't you shoot me, Stanley, the way you shoot dogs?" one night at supper, looking across the table at my father.

We acted as if she hadn't spoken.

Birds flew to the feeders, and, finding no food there, flew away, and in time they forgot why they had ever come. We still saw them in the bushes and trees, and heard them all around us, but none came to the feeders.

The time Thornton tossed a handful of seed on one of the feeders just as we were getting in the car, so he could tell Mama that he was taking care of the birds.

I didn't see my father take the notebooks, though I saw the splintered drawer where she had kept them.

I don't remember when I learned that he had burned them. I have an image of him flinging the notebooks into the incinerator but it doesn't feel like a real memory. It is perhaps only an imaginary picture that I invented to illustrate the remembered fact that he burned the notebooks, so it is not evidence that he burned them, standing there flinging them in one by one.

Though I know he did in fact burn them.

It was not as if she had forgotten the notebooks on a park bench somewhere, or left them in a taxi, as someone did just recently with a Stradivarius violin, I saw on television, in which case she would have had only herself to blame.

If she had left them on a bench or in a taxi it would be possible that one day in the future somebody would find them and be devastated.

The afternoon she came home I was on the front porch. Gracie heard them first. She lifted her head from her paws, pricked her ears, and padded down the steps to the yard, where she stood listening, and then I heard the car turning in from the highway. It had rained hard in the night, and when they came to a puddle Papa gunned the engine so as not to get bogged down in the middle. The car went into a huge puddle and tipped and wallowed, and the engine roared and it climbed out, I could tell just by the sound of it. The dogs ran barking down the road to greet them and escorted them back, racing in circles around the car, nipping at the tires. Papa stopped the car in front of the house and got out. "Goddamn dogs," he said, kicking them away.

I came down the steps. I didn't say anything or look directly at her.

She was thinner. Never buxom, she had melted away. Her hair, which was beginning to grow out again, was standing up in spikes. She looked like a little old man.

She knelt and let the dogs come around her, wriggling and wet.

She stood up. She said, "What dog is this?"

It was jumping up against her, it was nearly as tall as Gracie. Papa pushed it away with his foot. "Why that's Gracie's puppy," he said.

Edward came down and held the puppy. He didn't look at Mama. He talked to the puppy so as not to look at her. "That's Mama," he said, kneeling by the dog and fluffing its ears, "That's Mama."

Mama looked perplexed. She said, "What time is it?"

We had television now, in the library, all of us there at night looking at it.

I remember walking on the dikes, the cattails, brown and broken, barely visible on either side, and hearing the quivering voices of ducks murmuring in the fog. I don't know when that was. I have no feeling of my own size in this memory, standing alone on a dike, listening to the mewing and whimpering of the ducks and feeling the terribly cold dark water on either side.

I remember an impenetrable blackness coming at me from the cold dark water visible through the cattails.

I remember coming out of the cold into the warm house and sitting with the others and watching television.

The time she stood by the sideboard at suppertime and drew on a notepad that we kept by the telephone, glancing over at us from time to time, while we went on eating and pretended not to notice what she was doing. She came over and placed the drawing in the center of the table where we could all get a good look at it, but no one looked at it and no one took potatoes because the bowl of potatoes was next to the drawing. It was not her first drawing since coming back, so we knew how it would turn out: a table tilted at a crazy angle, stick figures seated at it, scarcely recognizable as human beings, the whole thing just a scribble, like something done by a talentless child.

The time my mother stood on the upper porch looking out across the yard, speaking to my father who was seated behind her but not turning to face him, as if talking to the trees. "You have destroyed my soul," she said, her voice cold and flat with hatred, "I will never forgive you."

Later, when only the two of us were left at Spring Hope, I sat with her on the porch glider. The cushions of the glider were covered in a plastic material. I remember my legs and back sweating and sticking to the plastic when I moved. Chameleons crept along the banisters, hunting flies. Mama hummed to herself.

When she had gone back inside, I would lie down on the glider. An oak tree rose and fell on the other side of the banister, moving up and down with short, quick jerks, different from the sweeping rise and fall of the magnolia from the hammock that had rotted away and that I would sometimes think about when I lay there sweating on the plastic of the glider, beginning to remember.

Hour after hour I heard the squeaking of the glider. The times I woke up in the night and heard it.

We fed stray dogs together. Mangy, sick, skeletal, some of them when they came, they followed us everywhere, cringing, grateful. After she died, I let them sleep in the house, but I never gave them names, knowing I wouldn't keep them. I couldn't stop myself from thinking "three legs," "blacky," "one eye," and so on, sorting them in my mind, but I never taught those names to the dogs.

The night I was awakened by the noise of breaking glass, the dogs barking and whining, when two teenage boys stood outside in the moonlight and threw rocks at my windows.

Walking around the house with Thornton, I looked at everything, thinking I won't see the sideboard again, I won't see the kitchen again, and so forth, and watching for broken glass, stepping around those places. Thornton walked right over the glass, grinding it with his shoes, and I remember thinking that of us all he was the one best equipped for life.

Maria thinks she will see her parents when she gets to heaven.

Imagine.

If I envision meeting my mother now, meeting her as she was at the end, as I am now, I get a picture of a vast green field and two crazy old ladies rushing madly across it into each other's arms.

I think my mother really was extravagant, and it was this, her artist's soul, as she would have called it, that undid her finally.

She saw the sky reflected in the window glass and flew into it.

I have now come to a point beyond which I think there is no point going on, no further points of any significance, I mean, to get to and stand on and feel that I have arrived somewhere. I don't know where time has gone.

# COFFEE HOUSE PRESS

THE MISSION OF COFFEE HOUSE PRESS is to publish exciting, vital, and enduring authors of our time; to delight and inspire readers; to contribute to the cultural life of our community; and to enrich our literary heritage. By building on the best traditions of publishing and the book arts, we produce books that celebrate imagination, innovation in the craft of writing, and the many authentic voices of the American experience.

Visit us at coffeehousepress.org.

LITERATURE
is not the same thing as
PUBLISHING

# FUNDER ACKNOWLEDGMENTS

COFFEE HOUSE PRESS is an independent, nonprofit literary publisher. All of our books, including the one in your hands, are made possible through the generous support of grants and donations from corporate giving programs, state and federal support, family foundations, and many individuals that believe in the transformational power of literature. We receive major operating support from Amazon, the Bush Foundation, the Jerome Foundation, the McKnight Foundation, the National Endowment for the Arts—a federal agency, and Target. Our activity is also made possible by the voters of Minnesota through a Minnesota State Arts Board Operating Support grant, thanks to a legislative appropriation from the arts and cultural heritage fund.

Coffee House Press receives additional support from many anonymous donors; the Elmer L. & Eleanor J. Andersen Foundation; the David & Mary Anderson Family Foundation; the Alexander Family Fund; the W. and R. Bernheimer Family Foundation; the E. Thomas Binger and Rebecca Rand Fund of the Minneapolis Foundation; the Patrick and Aimee Butler Family Foundation; the Buuck Family Foundation; the Carolyn Foundation; Dorsey & Whitney Foundation; Fredrikson & Byron, P.A.; the Lenfestey Family Foundation; the Nash Foundation;

the Rehael Fund of the Minneapolis Foundation; the Schwab Charitable Fund; Schwegman, Lundberg, Woessner & Kluth, P.A.; the Private Client Reserve of US Bank; the Archie D. & Bertha H. Walker Foundation; and the Wells Fargo Foundation of Minnesota.

# THE PUBLISHERS CIRCLE
# OF COFFEE HOUSE PRESS

THE PUBLISHERS CIRCLE is an exclusive group of individuals who make significant contributions to Coffee House Press's annual giving campaign. Understanding that a strong financial base is necessary for the press to meet the challenges and opportunities that arise each year, this group plays a crucial role in the success of our mission.

For more information about the Publishers Circle
and other ways to support Coffee House Press
books, authors, and activities,
please visit coffeehousepress.org/support
or contact us at: info@coffeehousepress.org.

**SAM SAVAGE** is the best-selling author of *Firmin: Adventures of a Metropolitan Lowlife*, *The Cry of the Sloth*, *Glass*, and *The Way of the Dog*, all from Coffee House Press. A finalist for the Barnes & Noble Discover Great New Writers Award, Savage holds a PhD in philosophy from Yale University and resides in Madison, Wisconsin.